Feivel's Flying Horses

In loving memory of my father Sumner, and to my mother Ellie
who brought me to the carousel in Hull. – H.S.H.

To my mom, Billie van der Sterre – J.v.d.S.

Kar-Ben Publishing
A division of Lerner Publishing Group, Inc.
241 First Avenue North
Minneapolis, MN 55401 U.S.A
1-800-4KARBEN
www.karben.com

Library of Congress Cataloging-in-Publication Data

Hyde, Heidi Smith.
  Feivel's flying horses / by Heidi Smith Hyde ; illustrated by Johanna van der Sterre.
    p. cm.
  Summary: A Jewish immigrant who is saving money to bring his wife and children to join him in America creates ornate horses for a carousel on Coney Island, one for each member of his family.
  ISBN 978–0–7613–3957–1 (lib. bdg. : alk. paper)
  [1. Merry-go-round—Fiction. 2. Merry-go-round horses—Fiction. 3. Wood carving—Fiction. 4. Jews—Fiction. 5. Coney Island (New York, N.Y.)—Fiction.] I. Sterre, Johanna van der, ill. II. Title.
  PZ7.H9677Fe 2010
  [E]—dc22   2008033480

Manufactured in the United States of America
1 — VI — 2/1/11

Feivel's Flying Horses

By Heidi Smith Hyde

Illustrated by Johanna van der Sterre

KAR-BEN
PUBLISHING

Feivel came to America with five dollars in his pocket. He had to leave his wife Goldie and his four children behind when he crossed the sea in search of a better life.

"Don't worry, Papa. I will protect the family while you are gone," said Hershel, his proud, oldest son.

"And I will carve wood to earn extra money," said Shmuel, his gentle, youngest boy.

"I will dance to lift Mama's spirits," said Sasha, his little prima ballerina.

Lena, only a baby, was too young to even say goodbye.

Feivel knew it would be months, even years before he could earn enough money to arrange passage for his family. By the time they were reunited, Lena would probably be a young lady and Shmuel a grown man.

In the Old Country, Feivel, his father, and his grandfather had been wood carvers. They had carved the ornate reading desks that held the Torah scrolls, and the fearsome lions that guarded the holy arks in synagogues throughout their province.

In New York, he found work as a furniture maker on the Lower East Side. Instead of carving lions and eagles, Feivel spent his days making tables, chairs, and dressers. In his spare time, he carved combs for fashionable ladies. It was hard work, but Feivel didn't mind. With each finished piece, he knew he was one step closer to sending for his family.

One day his cousin Mikhael suggested an outing.

"On the beach in Brooklyn there is an amusement park called Coney Island, with games of chance, Ferris wheels, and fortune tellers. They say there are so many electric lights that at night it glows like a million stars!"

Fortune tellers? Glittering lights? Feivel had never heard of such a place. "I don't think so, Mikhael. I need to save my pennies."

PARKWAY · BOWERY ·

HUSBAND STREETCAR

38

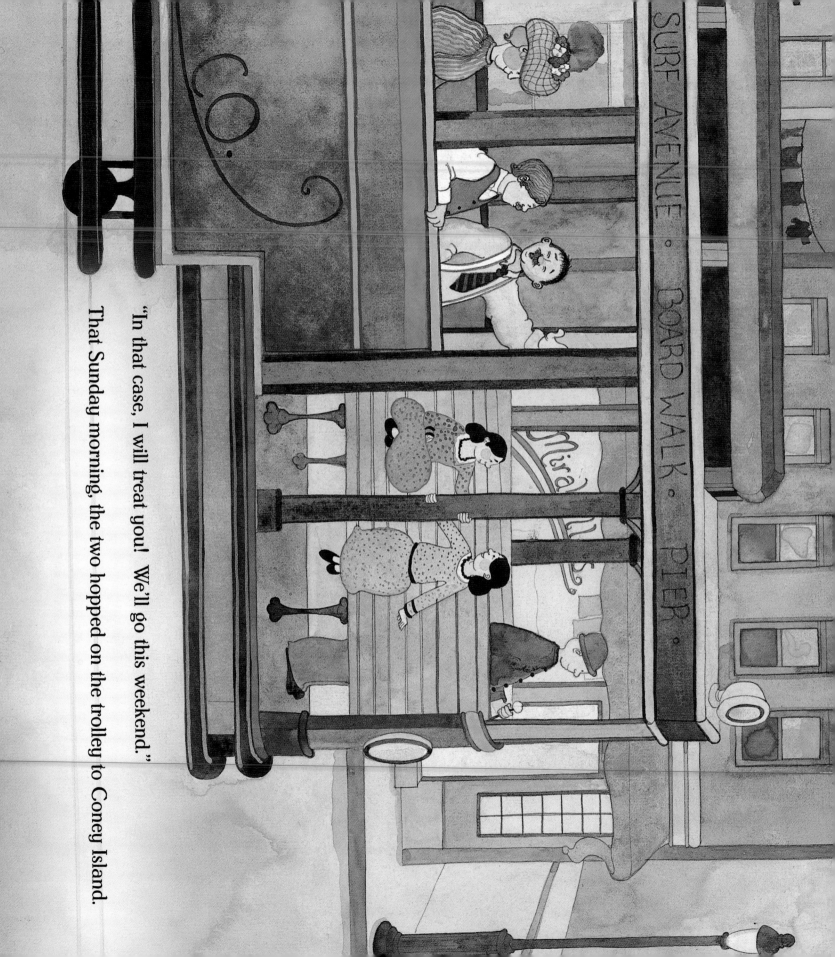

"In that case, I will treat you! We'll go this weekend."

That Sunday morning, the two hopped on the trolley to Coney Island.

As he stepped off the trolley, Feivel pinched himself to make sure he wasn't dreaming. Food stands, dance halls, and game parlors lined the boardwalk. He had never seen so many smiling faces.

Feivel gazed in wonderment at the colorful clowns and fortune tellers who roamed the streets. For five cents you could throw a ball into a hoop and win a giant purple doll. Right before his eyes, a man was being shot out of a cannon. Children on the roller coaster shrieked with excitement.

In the distance, Feivel heard organ music. He followed
the sound to a magnificent wooden carousel.
Its beautifully carved horses seemed to leap through
the air. Each creature, adorned with its sparkling jewels,
flashing buckles, and flowing ribbons, looked like
something out of the most wonderful dream.

Feivel remembered a music box he had seen as a child.
When it was opened, a glittering carousel appeared,
and horses danced round and round to the music.

"Come, Feivel. Let's get something to eat. I'm hungry," said Mikhael.

But Feivel was unable to tear himself away. Gazing at the brilliantly-painted chariots with their gold and silver leaf, he thought,"How I wish I could create something like this with my chisel and brush... something that children would cherish."

RED

And that's when he saw the sign:
Wanted: Experienced Wood Carver.
Rushing into the shop, Feivel applied
for the job and was hired.

WANTED

Experienced
Wood Carver

APPLY WITHIN

CONEY ISLAND
CAROUSELS
~Matriarson

As chief apprentice to the owner, Mr. Sumner Nathanson, Feivel was entrusted with the task of carving and embellishing the horses for the next Coney Island carousel.

As he worked, Feivel sang songs from the old country.

> Tumbala, tumbala, tumbalalaika
> Tumbalalaika, happy we'll be.

"What are you singing?" asked Avram, a younger apprentice.

"It's a love song I sang to Goldie when we first met," Feivel answered, wistfully.

Remembering his wife's silky hair, Feivel put the finishing touches on his first horse, a glorious creature with a long, golden mane as bright as sunshine.

"I shall call this horse Goldie," he announced. Then he carved her name in tiny letters beneath the saddle. He hoped Mr. Nathanson wouldn't mind.

He thought of his son Hershel as he carved the next horse, a restless beast whose speed and power made him stand out. "My eldest son is a proud young man," he told Avram. "Make sure you paint this horse a regal blue color."

It took Feivel a long time to complete his third horse, a kind, gentle creature. He etched deer in its bridle in honor of Shmuel, his youngest son, whose days were spent in the forest, carving wood.

Day and night, Feivel toiled away in the carousel shop, carving, sanding, painting and chiseling. On Shabbat, he rested. Sometimes he went to synagogue and sang blessings and prayers. The closer he came to completing his carousel, the louder he sang.

His next horse was festooned with flowers and ribbons.

"My Sasha is a dancer," Feivel told Avram, "so lively and so graceful… always pirouetting across the floor. Someday she will be a prima ballerina… you shall see!"

But Lena's horse was the most striking of all…Lena, his precious baby, whose laughing eyes shone like gemstones. One by one, Feivel cemented hundreds of glass jewels onto the horse until it glittered like the sun. Then he carved her name in tiny letters beneath the saddle.

"For my sweet baby, who is no longer a baby," he said with a sigh.

It took Feivel three years to complete the carousel. Cousin Mikhael and his family came to watch as Mr. Nathanson turned it on for the very first time.

"Papa, look at the horses fly round and round," shouted Mikhael's son. "Cousin Feivel's carousel is a circle that never ends!"

Tears glistened in Feivel's eyes as his beautiful horses galloped gracefully in the air, among them Goldie, Hershel, Shmuel, Sasha, and Lena. Some of the horses were gentle and some were fierce. Some spoke of happiness and love, some of sadness and loss.

"Aren't you going to ride the carousel, Feivel?" asked Mr. Nathanson.

Feivel shook his head. "No thank you, Mr. Nathanson. I prefer to wait until my wife and four children are here to enjoy it with me. With the wages you've paid me, I've saved enough money to send for my family."

And when, at last, Feivel's family arrived in America, they rode the carousel together, and the circle was complete.

Historical Note

For children nothing is more magical than riding a carousel, and it may surprise many readers to learn that some of the most beautiful carousel horses in America were carved by Jewish immigrants.

With the emergence of amusement parks such as Brooklyn's Coney Island, the carousel industry flourished in the late 1800s. This coincided with a wave of East European Jewish immigrants who came to America's shores in the late 19th century to escape persecution. The newcomers brought with them many skills, among them wood carving. Craftsmen, such as Marcus Charles Illions, an immigrant from Lithuania, made a living in the Old World carving synagogue arks, with fearsome lions and other three-dimensional creatures. In America, his talent found new expression in the magnificent carousel horses he created for Coney Island. Illions, an observant Jew, often carved his name in the bodies of his horses.

Yiddish-speaking immigrants Solomon Stein and Harry Goldstein, also wood carvers by trade, established a carousel shop in Brooklyn. During their lifetime they fashioned 17 carousels, some with up to six rows of horses. Charles Carmel, another Jewish immigrant, was known for his animated horses whose bodies sparkled with hundreds of glass jewels.

Through their work, these imaginative wood carvers bridged the transition between the Old World and the New, creating a new art form that was to delight generations of children.

Source: *Gilded Lions and Jeweled Horses: The Synagogue to the Carousel by Murray Zimiles, © 2007 American Folk Art Museum and Brandeis University Press*

About Author/Illustrator

Heidi Smith Hyde is a graduate of Brandeis University and Harvard Graduate School of Education. She is the Director of Education of Temple Sinai in Brookline, Massachusetts. Her first book, *Mendel's Accordion*, illustrated by Johanna van der Sterre, was the winner of the 2007 Sugarman Family Award for Best Jewish Children's Book. Heidi and her husband, Martin, live in Chestnut Hill with their two college age sons.

Johanna van der Sterre studied illustration at the Savannah College of Art and Design. From her cozy little home in the woods of upstate New York, she crafts her paintings with ink line and watercolors. She lives with her husband, Joseph, and two very bouncy dogs, Ernie and Rudy. Johanna is usually out running the trails with her dogs. And when Ernie and Rudy are satisfied that they have seen all there is to see, they let Johanna come back home to paint. This is her second book with author Heidi Smith Hyde.